Oh, My Darling, Clementine

Retold by BLAKE HOENA

Illustrated by TOM HEARD

CANTATA
LEARNING

WWW.CANTATALEARNING.COM

CANTATA
LEARNING

Published by Cantata Learning
1710 Roe Crest Drive
North Mankato, MN 56003
www.cantatalearning.com

Library of Congress Control Number: 2015932813
Hoena, Blake
    Oh, My Darling, Clementine / retold by Blake Hoena; Illustrated by Tom Heard
    Series: Tangled Tunes
    Audience: Ages: 3–8; Grades: PreK–3
    Summary: Follow a rugged cowboy and his sweet cow, Clementine, as the classic
folk song "Oh, My Darling, Clementine" gets a new twist for young readers.
    ISBN: 978-1-63290-357-0 (library binding/CD)
    ISBN: 978-1-63290-488-1 (paperback/CD)
    ISBN: 978-1-63290-518-5 (paperback)
    1. Stories in rhymes. 2. Cowboys—fiction. 3. Cows—fiction.

Book design, Tim Palin Creative
Editorial direction, Flat Sole Studio
Music direction, Elizabeth Draper
Music arranged and produced by Steven C Music

Printed in the United States of America in North Mankato, Minnesota.
122015   0326CGS16

ACCESS THE MUSIC!

SCAN CODE WITH MOBILE APP

CANTATALEARNING.COM

Have you ever lost something that was important to you? That is what happens to the **cowboy** in this story. He loses his cow, Clementine. Can you find her?

Now turn the page and get ready to sing along!

In a **pasture**, in a **prairie**,
walking down a railroad line,
lived a cowboy with a big hat
and his cow named Clementine.

Oh, my darling, oh, my darling, oh, my darling, Clementine. You are lost and gone forever. I'm so sorry, Clementine.

She was white with big black spots and a bell around her neck.

She made enough milk in a day
to fill up forty buckets.

Now the cow and her cowboy
together roamed the wide prairies.

She would graze on the green grass while he chewed a stalk of wheat.

Then one day the cowboy came upon a **burger** place.

He ordered a beef **patty**,
and Clementine ran away.

In a pasture, in a prairie,
walking down a railroad line,
lived a cowboy with a big hat
and his cow named Clementine.

19

Oh, my darling, oh, my darling,
oh, my darling, Clementine.
You are lost and gone forever.
I'm so sorry, Clementine.

SONG LYRICS
Oh, My Darling, Clementine

In a pasture, in a prairie,
walking down a railroad line,
lived a cowboy with a big hat
and his cow named Clementine.

Oh, my darling, oh, my darling,
oh, my darling, Clementine.
You are lost and gone forever.
I'm so sorry, Clementine.

She was white with big black spots
and a bell around her neck.

She made enough milk in a day
to fill up forty buckets.

Oh, my darling, oh, my darling,
oh, my darling, Clementine.
You are lost and gone forever.
I'm so sorry, Clementine.

Now the cow and her cowboy
together roamed the wide prairies.

She would graze on the green grass
while he chewed a stalk of wheat.

Then one day the cowboy
came upon a burger place.

He ordered a beef patty,
and Clementine ran away.

In a pasture, in a prairie,
walking down a railroad line,
lived a cowboy with a big hat
and his cow named Clementine.

Oh, my darling, oh, my darling,
oh, my darling, Clementine.
You are lost and gone forever.
I'm so sorry, Clementine.

Oh, My Darling, Clementine

Americana
Steven C Music

Verse

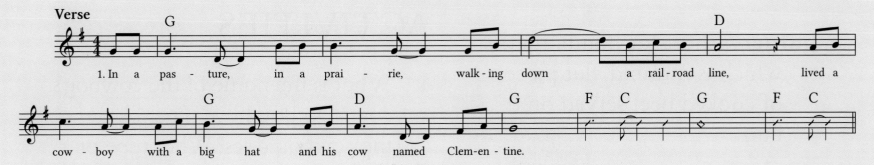

1. In a pas - ture, in a prai - rie, walk-ing down a rail-road line, lived a

cow - boy with a big hat and his cow named Clem-en- tine.

Chorus

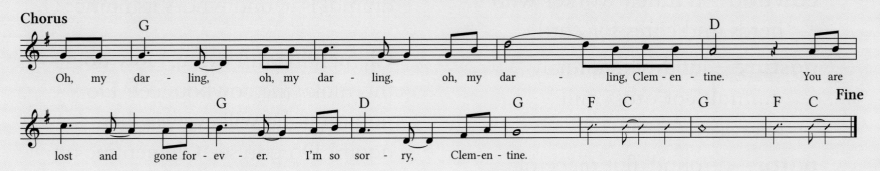

Oh, my dar - ling, oh, my dar - ling, oh, my dar - ling, Clem-en- tine. You are

lost and gone for - ev - er. I'm so sor - ry, Clem-en- tine.

Fine

Verse 2
She was white with big black spots
and a bell around her neck.
She made enough milk in a day
to fill up forty buckets.

Verse 3
Now the cow and her cowboy
together roamed the wide prairies.
She would graze on the green grass
while he chewed a stalk of wheat.

Chorus

Verse 4

4. Then one day the cow - boy came up - on a burg-er place.

He or - dered a beef pat - ty, and Clem-en- tine ran a - way.

D. C. Al Fine

GLOSSARY

burger—short for hamburger, which is a round, flat piece of cooked beef served on a bun

cowboy—a ranch worker who herds and cares for cattle

pasture—land where farm animals eat grass and exercise

patty—a round, flat piece of cooked beef

prairie—a large area of rolling grassland with few or no trees

GUIDED READING ACTIVITIES

1. What is the name of the cowboy's cow? Do you have a pet like the cowboy does? What type of animal is it, and what's its name?

2. Clementine ran away. How does this make the cowboy feel? Do you think he will ever see her again? Do you see Clementine on every page of the story?

3. Clementine is white and black. What other animals are white and black? Can you draw them?

TO LEARN MORE

Doyle, Sheri. *Cows*. North Mankato, MN: Capstone Press, 2013.

Gibbs, Maddie. *Cows*. New York: PowerKids Press, 2015.

Stiefel, Chana. *Cows on the Family Farm*. Berkeley Heights, NJ: Enslow Elementary, an imprint of Enslow Publishers, 2013.

Taus-Bolstad, Stacy. *From Grass to Milk*. Minneapolis: Lerner Publications, 2013.